Text copyright © 2018 by Robert Wilson

Illustrations copyright © by Robert Wilson

First paperback edition in this format 2018

ISBN 978-17-1819-192-1 (paperback)

Learn more about Robert Wilson on Instagram at

@jiujitsuandme

All our dreams can come true,
If we have the courage to pursue them.
- Walt Disney

"C'mon, Bobby!" Mom called from downstairs. "It's time for school!" Bobby had been dreading this day all summer long. He loved summer. He played games with his friends, went camping with his family and got to visit his grandparents. The summer holidays were his favorite time of the year. "Bobby, let's go," Mom called again.

"Coming!" Bobby replied with a sigh.

Bobby put his school bag on and tiptoed down the stairs. The thought of school made him anxious. He knew that he would be picked last for sports. He found it hard to focus on his studies and most of all, he didn't have many friends there. Bobby wanted to be liked, but found it very hard to express himself in school.

Once he arrived, Bobby strolled into his new classroom.
Mr. Miller was Bobby's new third-grade teacher. Bobby immediately
liked Mr. Miller. He was very polite and confident. His lessons were fun
and exciting, but what Bobby enjoyed most was Mr. Miller's stories
of jiu-jitsu. Mr. Miller was a
black belt jiu-jitsu instructor
in the local jiu-jitsu academy.

Every summer, he trained and competed all around the world. Bobby was fascinated by his dedication and love of the sport.

That night, Bobby lay in bed thinking about jiu-jitsu. He imagined traveling around the world and doing competitions, just like Mr. Miller.

The next morning on the way to school,
Bobby said: "Mom, I want to try jiu-jitsu."
Upon hearing this, his mom was very excited. "Let me
see what I can do Bobby," Mom said with a smile.

Bobby listened intently to Mr. Miller's jiu-jitsu stories, and this made him want to be more engaged with what they were doing in class. Unfortunately, at lunch, he would still sit alone, and in P.E. he was always picked last for each sport. It wasn't that Bobby was terrible at sports, he just wasn't that interested.

After school, that day, Bobby's mom collected him with a big grin on her face. "Hey Bobby, I have a surprise for you," she said secretively. "Look what I got you." as she handed him a white jiu-jitsu uniform. Bobby's eyes opened wide in delight. "Thank you, thank you, thank you," he shouted while jumping for joy.

That evening was Bobby's first lesson. He put on his new uniform with anticipation. He took a deep breath and nervously stepped on the mats. Mr. Miller smiled when he saw Bobby and quickly introduced him to the class. Bobby was surprised. The class was so much fun. Not only did he learn some interesting techniques, but they also played fun games. The kids were very welcoming to Bobby, which made him feel accepted and comfortable.

Bobby began to train every day after school. He loved that he was learning jiu-jitsu, but most of all, he now had lots of friends. Bobby couldn't be happier.

"How do you find the training Bobby?" asked Mr. Miller one day after class.
"Good sir, but I don't feel I'm getting any better," Bobby answered.
"It takes many years to get better at jiu-jitsu," Mr. Miller said while smiling.
"But answer me this question, do you enjoy training?"
"Yes sir, I have many new friends, and we have lots of fun," Bobby replied enthusiastically.
"That's the most important thing. You will get better the more you train.
So, just enjoy the journey."

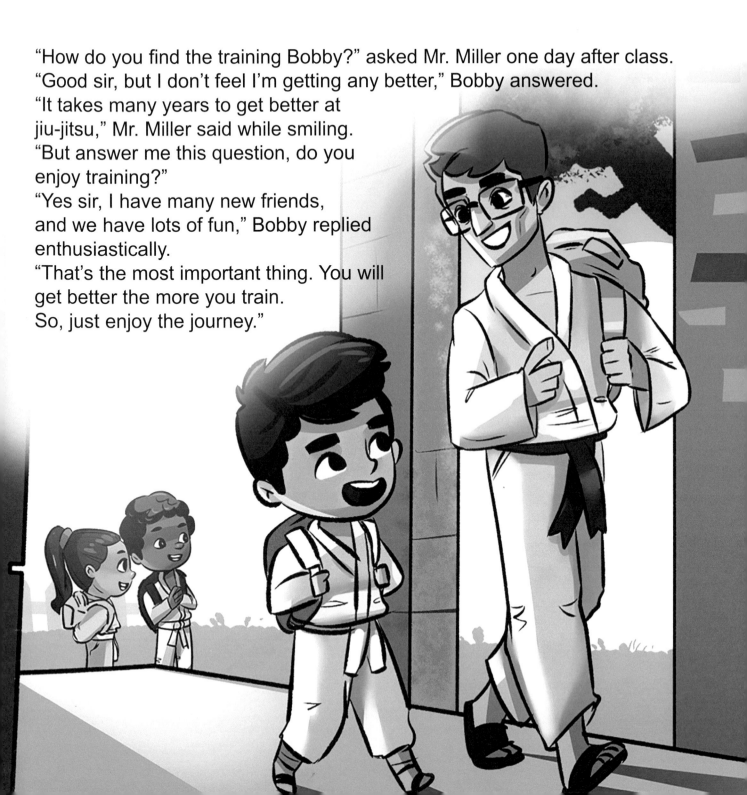

One evening after class, Mr. Miller asked Bobby "Would you like to join the jiu-jitsu competition at the end of the month?"

Bobby was scared. He thought about all the times he had lost at sports in school. "No sir, I wouldn't be very good," replied Bobby grimly.

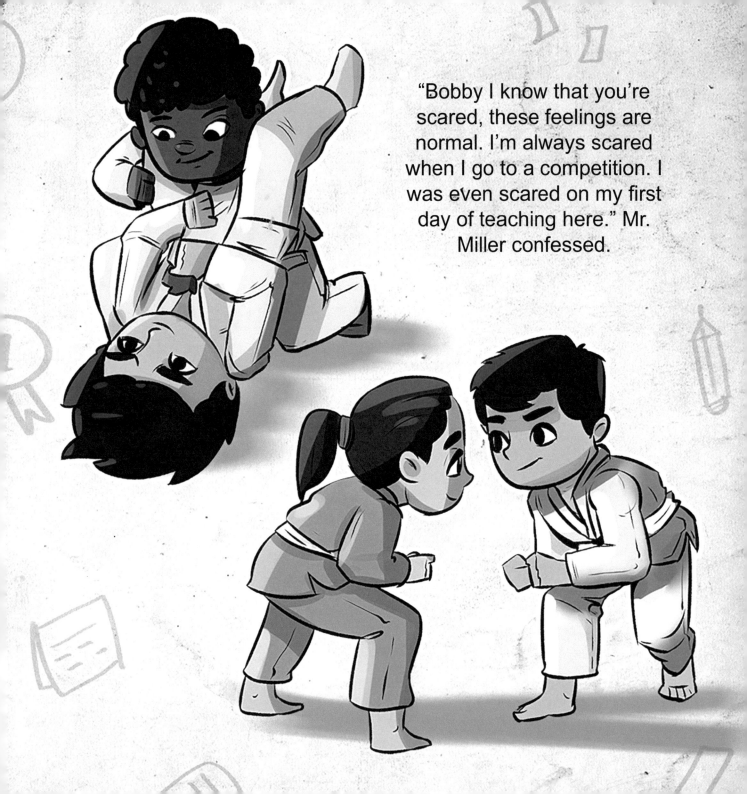

"Bobby I know that you're scared, these feelings are normal. I'm always scared when I go to a competition. I was even scared on my first day of teaching here." Mr. Miller confessed.

Bobby was shocked, how could Mr. Miller be scared? He was the most confident person he knew. "It's okay to be afraid. But, you cannot let fear stop you from doing anything. I promise, if you can conquer your fears, you can achieve anything."

"But what if I lose?" Bobby questioned while staring at the floor.

"Bobby," Mr. Miller said as Bobby shyly glanced up. "What if you win?"

After thinking about it, Bobby decided to enter the competition, which was only three weeks away. Bobby was determined to face his fear of competing and to do his very best. He worked hard in school every day by always listening and taking notes. He completed his homework immediately after school so that he could focus on his jiu-jitsu in the evening.

He realized that his grades improved, and better yet, he was making friends. Inspired by Mr. Miller, some of his classmates also started jiu-jitsu, and they would sit with Bobby at lunchtime to talk about training and the competition. He even enjoyed P.E. more and wasn't always picked last. Jiu-jitsu was changing his life.

The day of the competition soon arrived, and Bobby knew he had done all he could to prepare. Now it was time to do his best. He was nervous, but he remembered what Mr. Miller had told him—"If you can conquer your fears, then you can achieve anything."

Before long, Bobby heard his name being called. He took a deep breath, stood up, straightened his uniform and walked confidently onto the mat. The match began. The other boy was bigger than he was, and a lot more experienced.

The boy used a takedown technique to knock Bobby to the mat; this gave him two points. Bobby remembered his training and stayed calm under his opposition. Using a well-practiced series of moves, he was able to get back to the standing position again.

The boy used the same takedown to bring Bobby to the mat for the second time. There were only a few seconds left on the clock, and Bobby was losing—four points to zero. He realized he was not nervous anymore. Bobby then saw an opportunity and executed a sweep perfectly, giving him two points. He managed to hold the top position until the match ended.

Bobby was ecstatic. Although he did not win, he had conquered his fear of competing. "I did it, Mom, I competed, and I got a takedown," Bobby exclaimed while jumping into her arms.

"I am so proud of you Bobby," Mom replied as she hugged him tightly. "As long as you've got passion and are willing to work hard, you can do anything you want in this world."

Bobby grinned. "Time to start training for the next competition."

Made in United States
Troutdale, OR
10/27/2023